The Lost Diary of King Henry VIII's Executioner

The Lost Diary of King Henry VIII's Executioner

Discovered by
Steve Barlow and Steve Skidmore
Illustrated by George Hollingworth

Collins
An imprint of HarperCollinsPublishers

First published in Great Britain by Collins in 1997

7 9 10 8

Collins is an imprint of HarperCollins*Publishers* Ltd,
77-85 Fulham Palace Road, Hammersmith, London W6 8JB

Text © Steve Barlow and Steve Skidmore 1997
Illustrations © George Hollingworth 1997
Cover illustration © Martin Chatterton

ISBN 0 00 694555 4

The authors assert the moral right to be
identified as the authors of this work

Printed and bound in Great Britain by
Caledonian International Book Manufacturing Ltd,
Glasgow, G64

MESSAGE TO READERS

During building work on a cottage in a village near Richmond, Surrey, a small lead box was discovered hidden in the foundations of the house.

When the box was opened, it was found to contain several small notebooks, carefully preserved but obviously very old.

Historians who examined the books were delighted to discover that they seemed to be the diaries and scrapbook cuttings of one Watkyn 'Chopper' Smith, chief executioner at the court of King Henry VIII.

They have been authenticated by Professor F. Orgery of Bognor University and Watt A. Lyer, the well-known American expert on Tudor times.

Steve Barlow and Steve Skidmore, who originally found the notebooks, have selected the most interesting of the diary entries for publication which reveal astonishing details about life in the Tudor Court and fascinating glimpses of Henry VIII, the man behind the legend.

This diary belongs to:

Name: Watkyn Smith

Addresses: The Tower Of London
The Palace Of Richmond
Hampton Court

Date of birth: 28/06/1491

Occupation: Executioner/Torturer

Doctor: Who needs them!

Dentist/Barber: Cruncher Harris

Employer's Name: King Henry VIII

Address: As above

If Unavailable: ~~Queen Catherine,~~ ~~Queen Anne,~~ ~~Queen Jane,~~ ~~Queen Anne,~~ ~~Queen Catherine,~~ Queen Catherine

Hobbies: Chopping, hanging, drawing, quartering, burning at the stake, wild flower collecting and being kind to animals.

Favourite food: Chops and chips

Clubs: Three, all with nails in

Motto: Chop 'til you drop!

23rd April, 1509

Here I am, first day in the new job, chief executioner to His Majesty, King Henry VIII.

King Henry asked for me personally. No idea why. I asked him but he just grinned and tapped the side of his nose. I suppose he'll tell me when he's ready.

We're staying at the Royal Palace of Richmond at the moment. It isn't half big! I'm a bit nervous about the chopping, not having done it before. All right, I've chopped the heads off flowers. I've even squashed frogs and swatted the odd insect in my time, but I reckon chopping human heads off is a bit different! Still, the pay's good – four pounds a year – and I get an axe allowance and hood thrown in. I dare say I'll soon get into the swing of it.

24th April, 1509

I went in to see the King after breakfast this morning. He was having a light snack: lark's tongues, a few stewed sparrows, a roast pigeon or two.

He thought Watkyn Smith was a daft name for an executioner. He said I should call myself Slasher, or Scragger, or Chopper.

"Righto, Guv'nor," I said.

I quite fancy being called 'Chopper' Smith. It's got a bit of a ring to it, I reckon.

test run.

5th June, 1509

The Guv'nor is getting married before he gets crowned. He's sent me an invitation to the wedding and the coronation. A messenger brought it round this morning.

Invytation

Watkyn ('Chopper') Smith

You are invited to join the King on the occasion
of his marriage to Catherine of Aragon,
on June 11th in the Year of our Lord 1509,
at the Private Chapel, Greenwich.
You are also invited to attend his coronation on
23rd June at Westminster Abbey, followed by
a reception (in Westminster Hall if wet).

Bring a bottle

White ruffs to be worn   RSVP

You could have knocked me down with a feather! I reckon it's going to be a month of parties and drinking!

ye Sonne

England's favourite Dailey

12th June, 1509   Still only Five Groats

Gotcha!

Hunky Henry, everybody's favourite monarch, got splyced yesterday to curvy Kate of Aragon. In front of a few selected guests, the passionate Prince married his Spanish sweetharte.

Royal watchers will remember that tragic Catherine was married to Henry's brother, Arthur, before he died. She and Henry have been engaged since he was twelve years old and she was seventeen, proving that our Harry isn't one to rushe into things!

Petite Catherine (23) said after the wedding, "I am so 'appee!" Asked how he felt, Henry said, "I would choose her for a wife above all others."

The King will celebrate his marriage with jousts, feasting and merriemaking. After his stick-in-the-mud dad, this is goode news!

Ye Sonne says, "You're a pal, Hal!"

23rd June, 1509

What a day! I couldn't get in the Abbey for the coronation, but I watched the Guv'nor and his queen-to-be go in. What a laugh! As they walked along a bit of carpet, people came down like rats and chopped it up for souvenirs! Then all the toffs walking behind in the procession kept tripping up in the holes.

After that, it was the wedding feast. I got into that! What fantastic grub. We had roast swan, roast heron, roast venison and roast pig, with all the trimmings. I think we had roast stork, as well, but I can't tell stork from bittern. Anyway, good job I'm not a vegetarian – I'd have been dead hungry!

26th June, 1509

Went to watch the jousting today. What a to-do! They had two teams, Lady Pallas's Knights and Lady Diana's Knights. (Why they couldn't call them something simple like 'United' or 'City', I don't know.) Anyway, they hacked away at each other like nobody's business, and some of them lost their tempers. They were supposed to be jousting for a gold lance and a crystal shield, but the whole thing turned into a free-for-all and I don't know who won or even if anybody did.

3rd September, 1510

The Guv'nor popped in this morning to tell me a couple of lads needed chopping. To be honest, I was quite chuffed when I found out who they were; none other than Sir Richard Empson and Edmund Dudley. They'd been very unpopular ministers of the Guv'nor's dad. The Guv'nor had had them arrested the first day he took the throne which made him very popular with everyone (except Empson and Dudley, of course).

We had a nice day for it, big crowd, all singing, "'Ere we go, 'ere we go, 'ere we go..." I didn't mind that, but I could have done without everybody pointing at my axe and chanting, "Come and have a go if you think you're hard enough", and the yells of "He's behind you!" when Dudley put his neck on the block.

Empson was making his way up the scaffold, when he staggered a bit and said, "Sorry, I haven't got a head for heights."

"Don't worry," I replied, "soon you're not going to have a head for anything!"

That got a big laugh. I reckon I should be a jester!

10th September, 1510

Fame at last! Some bloke from the *Toppers' Times* asked me to do an advert for some of their kit:

I did all right out of this!

2nd September, 1511

The Guv'nor's keeping himself busy with his plans for the Royal Navy. He's going to build some new ships, with two decks and seventy guns apiece. He showed me some drawings. The new ships are bigger than anything France or Spain has got, and look the business.

15th May, 1512
We're at war!

The Guv'nor made a claim to the French throne but old Louis XII said "Non", so the Army's setting off for Calais to sort the French out, and everybody's cheering and knitting woolly hats for the troops.

1st November, 1512

Not much news from France. It seems the Guv'nor isn't in too much of a hurry to find the French to start fighting. The Pope says Louis isn't King any more, and he's given France to the Guv'nor. This is all very well, but whatever the Pope says, Louis is still in Paris and our army is still partying in Calais, not likely to stir before the winter.

Meanwhile, it isn't half boring around here.

> Calais
>
> Par Bateau Carte Postale
>
> Dear Chopper
> Weather continues
> fine. This is a
> picture of where
> we are but you
> can't see our
> camp. It's just to
> the left. Henry Rex
>
> Chopper Smith,
> Tower of London,
> England.

ye Sonne

England's favourite Dailey

16th August 1513   **Still only Six Groats**

Henry wins his spurs!

King Henry VIII today won his first battle, only a few miles from the field of Agincourt where King Henry V gave the French a good pasting nearly 100 years ago.

The frightened French showed no stomache for the fight, and were soon running for their lives.

Ye Sonne says, "Nice One, Hal!"

The messengers who brought the news, said they still couldn't work out what happened in the battle. The French cavalry outnumbered our blokes by ten to one, but as soon as the fighting started they just chucked their swords away and scarpered. Apparently the French are calling it 'The Battle of the Spurs' because their cavalry ran away so fast!

15th September, 1513

Big job today – Edmund de la Pole, the Earl of Suffolk, no less!

The Queen sent for me this morning. She told me to take the Earl out of the dungeons and, as she put it, "'Ave ees 'ead off!"

I said I was only supposed to take orders from the Guv'nor. She lost her rag at that and did a lot of stamping about. She told me Henry had left her in charge, and if I didn't fancy the job, she could soon find someone who did. So I had to get on with it.

We had a big crowd, all shouting, "Hurry up! Chop, chop!" When I'd lopped off his head, everybody sang, "Oh, it's all gone quiet over there." Mind you, when the crowd started singing, "Oh there won't be many going home," you couldn't really argue, not if you were the ex-Earl of Suffolk anyway.

To be honest, I felt a bit sorry for the poor bloke. After all, he's been in the dungeons of the Tower of London since the Guv'nor's dad found out he was plotting against him in 1506. Still, orders are orders, so it was off with 'is 'ead and bye-bye Ed.

5th June, 1514

I met that jumped-up little squirt Thomas Wolsey this morning. I've never liked him. He's only the son of an Ipswich butcher, but he's really come up in the world. He's been made Archbishop of York! He told me Louis XII has decided to make peace with the new Pope, so the war with France is over. The Guv'nor's on his way home and his sister, Mary, is going to marry Louis as part of the peace treaty. Poor kid! She's only young, and Louis is over fifty and a right weed. Wonder how long he'll last?

3rd February, 1515
Bit of interesting reading in the paper this morning:

Sonne Gossipe

King Louis XII of France collapsed and dyed on the fyrst of Januarie, aftere eighty-two days...or to be more exact, eighty-two nights...of marriage to Mary, sister of our beloved King Henry. The word from the french court is that his laste wordes were, "Ooh, la, la!"

This puttes Mary in a bit of a spotte, as she is no longere Queene of france now Louis is deade. My sources indicate that she has been mayking eyes at Francis, Louis' nephew and heir, but he is not interested.

10th October, 1515

The Guv'nor came round today looking a bit sheepish. I could see there was something a bit different about him, but I couldn't think what it was. He looked down at his legs and coughed. My eyes followed his and – I let out a "Wup!"

The Guv'nor looked all anxious and said, "D'you think they're all right?"

His hose were as tight as if they'd been painted on. I said he looked very stylish and he went off looking pleased, leaving me to wonder what on earth made him want to look like an overweight turkey.

I found out later that the Guv'nor is dead jealous of Francis, the new King of France and some creep, to get in the Guv'nor's good books, told him he had better legs than Francis, so he's started showing them off. He's even changed the way he walks; he goes about with his feet splayed out to show off his muscles. He looks like a duck, waddling about the place, but I'm not going to tell him and nobody else is either. A right royal fashion victim!

17th December, 1515

I keep waiting for Thomas Wolsey to slip up, but the little squirt goes from strength to strength. First the Pope makes him a cardinal (last week he had all the toffs in court round his place bowing and scraping to his cardinal's hat!), and now the Guv'nor has made him Lord Chancellor, so he's got the top jobs in both the Church and the Government. I really don't know what the Guv'nor sees in him.

All this seems to be going to Wolsey's head, but one false move and something else will – my axe!

18th February, 1516

I knew as soon as the Guv'nor came in this evening that it wasn't good news. Everyone knew the Queen was expecting again, and we were all hoping that it would turn out all right this time.

He had a swig of sack, and I asked him if the baby had died.

"It's worse than that, Chopper," he said. "It's a girl."

5th March, 1516

I met the Royal Nursemaid out walking little Princess Mary. I had to stop and admire her. Then I looked at the baby – ugly little thing, even for a baby; face screwed up in temper, nasty sickly complexion. She screamed the place down (I didn't know I was that scary) and puked all over her pram.

"Lovely," I said.

I've been trying to cheer the Guv'nor up – after all, at least now he's got an heir and if the Queen has a boy next, *he'll* be the heir. The Guv'nor won't have it, he just mooches round looking gloomy and every time he sees the kid, he shudders.

20th May, 1520

I'm off to France! Not just me, of course. I reckon the Guv'nor's taking everybody but the palace cat (he hates that cat!). He got an invite from King Francis to come over for a summit meeting (which is just another way of saying big party). The Guv'nor is determined to outdo the French so he's taking five thousand of us to put on a good show. This is okay by me – if the Guv'nor wants to give us all a holiday with free wine and all the frog's legs we can eat, who am I to argue?

Tower of London
26th June, 1520

Dear Mum
Just got back from France; blimey, what a carry-on.

The Guv'nor and Francis had arranged to meet near Calais. They're calling the meeting 'The Field of the Cloth of Gold' because the Guv'nor had his tent made out of gold cloth!

The whole thing was just an excuse for the Guv'nor and Francis to try to outdo each other.

On the first day, the Guv'nor wore out six horses going over a thousand jumps. Talk about boring, but of course we all had to clap like mad.

Then it was archery, and the Guv'nor kept hitting the bull's eye from over 200 yards. He did pretty well in the jousting too.

The trouble was, all this success went to the Guv'nor's head. Before lunch, he sang out, "Brother, we will wrestle," and he grabbed Francis and started heaving and grunting away. The French started protesting that it wasn't fair, because the Guv'nor was bigger and heavier, but thirty seconds later the Guv'nor was flat on his back at the Queen's feet and our blokes were shouting "Foul!"

Of course, the Guv'nor had to laugh it off and congratulate Francis, but I saw the look they gave each other. Whatever you read in the papers about trust and understanding between our two nations, don't believe a word of it. The Guv'nor and Frank hate each other's guts and, if they get the excuse, they'll go to war faster than you can say, "two falls, two submissions or a knockout".

Your loving son,

Watkyn

17th May, 1521

Had to chop the Duke of Buckingham today. It was all that little rat Cardinal Wolsey's doing. Old Buckingham was a genuine royal (blue blood and all), which was one reason the crabby cardinal couldn't stand him. Wolsey accused him of treason, having tortured and bribed Buckingham's own servants into giving evidence against him. Then rigged the trial. The old boy didn't have a chance...

ye Sonne

Your Soarawaye Sonne

17th May, 1521   Still only Nine Groats

Buckingham Guilty

Edward Stafford, Duke of Buckingham, was today found guilty of plotting treason against the King's Majesty. Weeping, Buckingham's buddy, the Duke of Norfolk, read out the sentence. The traitor Buckingham will:

- be hanged by the neck
- be cut downe while still alive
- have his limbs amputated and caste into the flames
- have his bowels burnt before him★
- have his head smitten off
- have his body cut into quarters

In the end, Wolsey let him off with a regular beheading. Strange really, you'd think Wolsey would be keen on seeing Buckingham chopped to bits – his dad is a butcher after all.

Well, I did the business, but I can't say my heart was in it. I've got a special axe put aside for Cardinal Cowpat Wolsey. I'm keeping it blunt, on purpose.

11th October, 1521

I'm getting dead tired of hearing about this book of the Guv'nor's. It's called *The Golden Book*. According to Wolsey (who's read it, the creep), it's an attack on some German monk called Martin Luther who's going round saying the Church has got everything wrong, and rich people can't just buy their way out of hell by giving money to the Church. Actually, that sounds pretty good sense to me.

Anyway, the Pope's well chuffed with the Guv'nor and has given him a new title, 'Defender of the Faith'.

Henry VIII

18th August, 1523

Cardinal Cowpat is swanning about as if he owns the place, and he even wants to be the next Pope! The Guv'nor is getting fed-up with him and is going to make his old pal, Sir Thomas More, speaker of Parliament. More hates Wolsey, so he won't be getting all his own way from now on.

As for me, I just keep eyeing up Wolsey's neck, making sure he sees me doing it.

- Thomas Wolsey. -

10th March, 1524

The Guv'nor had a nasty accident today. Everyone's been telling him for years he should pack in jousting. He used to be really good at it, but he's not a young man anymore. But the Guv'nor won't have it. Today he insisted on having a tilt with Sir Charles Brandon, who's the best jouster in the business.

Well, they set off towards each other, but the Guv'nor had forgotten to drop his visor and Brandon's spear hit the Guv'nor smack on the head. Although it didn't kill him (luckily), it left the Guv'nor feeling fairly groggy.

This evening he came round with a bump on his bonce the size of a duck egg and while we drank a bottle of sack, he told me he was hanging up his sabots and taking up a more gentle pastime – music. Not before time, I reckon.

12th July, 1525

I wish the Guv'nor would go back to jousting! It's kinder on the ears than his music!

He came in with his lute to play his latest.

"What do you reckon?" he asked me when he'd finished. "I'm calling it 'Pinksleeves'."

I told him that it wasn't a bad tune (if I hadn't I'd soon be appearing on Top of the Chops) but the title was a bit dated.

"What's wrong with 'Pinksleeves'?" he asked.

"That colour's out of date, not in fashion."

He shrugged his shoulders and stared at my tunic. "Right Chopper. You're a man of fashion. Instead of 'Pinksleeves', I'll call it 'Greensleeves'." And with that he wandered off.

After he'd gone, I looked at my shirt. I thought it best not to tell the Guv'nor that the sleeves should be white. They are only green because it's where I wipe my nose.

1st November, 1525

I met Will Somers today. He's the Guv'nor's latest court fool. And 'fool' is the right word. He came in wearing a stupid hat with bells on it, and begun hopping and jigging all over the place.

"Hello, Chopper. I've heard that people at court don't like you," he said

"Why's that?" I asked, worried that I was in trouble.

"Because you give them a pain in the neck!" and he calls himself a jester! One more joke like that, and he'll be jester bit shorter than he was before!

13th June, 1526

The Guv'nor asked me today what I thought of Anne Boleyn. I said, without thinking, I'd heard she was a bit of a raver. The Guv'nor got all huffy and said he never listened to malicious gossip. Then a horrible thought struck me.

"You don't mean you fancy her, do you?" I blurted out. "I thought you..." I managed to stop myself there, which was just as well or I'd be on the rack by now, eight feet long and getting longer. I was about to say that I thought he was having a fling with Anne's sister, Mary (it was the talk of the court), and he'd already chatted up her mum, Elizabeth, though that was a few years ago. Talk about keeping it in the family!

The Guv'nor went into a royal rage. He said he needed another wife. What use had Catherine ever been to him?

Had she given him a son? No! All her children had died except that ugly little witch, Mary.

Speaking of witches, I said; Anne's got six fingers on her left hand. I suppose it could be useful being married to someone who could count to eleven without taking her shoes off, but my old gran used to say that anyone with extra toes or fingers is a witch.

Looking back on it, that probably wasn't a very clever thing to say. I thought the Guv'nor was going to explode. He gave me the sort of look he gives people just before he tells me to chop 'em. Whoops, I thought. He didn't say anything; just turned on his heel and walked away.

I reckon he's determined to get a new wife, but the problem is, he's going to have to get rid of the one he's got already! I also reckon I'd better come up with something to get back in the Guv'nor's good books pretty quickly, or the next neck on my block will be mine!

1st December, 1526

I popped in to see the Guv'nor this morning. He wouldn't let me in for ages, and when he did, he just growled, "What do you want?"

I said I'd thought of a way of getting rid of Catherine. I told him I'd been skimming through the Bible and had found a bit in it saying it was illegal to marry your brother's wife, which is what he'd done.

The Guv'nor asked me what I was getting at. I said there were only two ways he could get rid of the Queen (apart from chopping her):

1 - if he divorced her, or

2 - if he'd never been married to her in the first place.

The Guv'nor said he'd been married to Catherine for eighteen years.

"Not according to the Bible," I said. All he had to do was get the Pope to agree that his marriage was illegal. Then he could give Catherine the boot and marry Anne Boleyn.

He was all for it. He reckoned that Wolsey could sort it out with the Pope. And if the Pope wouldn't agree... well, that would be too bad for Wolsey.

I left him chuckling and rubbing his hands, so I reckon I've got away with it.

26th December, 1526

The Guv'nor gave me a few days off for giving him the plan to get rid of Catherine, so I nipped home for Christmas.

My mum's house seemed really poky compared to my flat in the Tower. Yes, the house has got a sturdy wooden frame, and the stick and plaster walls look nice, but there's only one room and the floor is covered in rushes that must be weeks old, they are that filthy. And the smell!

I told her to make a new hole for the privy and make it further away from the door.

"But what if I want to go in the night?" she said. "I'll have to walk too far!"

I reckon I might try and find her one of those privies that the courtiers keep under their beds for any night time urges.

3rd January, 1527

Will Somers came over today, still jigging and hopping about. He could tell I wasn't happy to see him.

"Just remember," he said. "There's something worse than being with a fool."

"What's that?" I asked.

"Fooling with a bee."

I don't know *why* the Guv'nor thinks he's funny.

3rd February, 1527

Went to Cruncher Harris, the barber surgeon, today. I walked into his shop and before I could say "Hello", two big blokes grabbed me and pushed me into a chair.

Then Cruncher forced my jaws open, stuffed a great pair of tongs into my mouth and pulled out one of my six remaining teeth.

I nearly shot through the roof – he hadn't even given me a swig of brandy first to numb the pain!

I couldn't say anything to him. I just left holding my jaw. And the worse thing about it all? I only went in there for a haircut! I reckon I'll have a word with the Guv'nor about making up a law that says surgeons are surgeons and barbers are barbers, so they can't take your teeth out or cut your leg off when all you want is a short back and sides.

Just wait till Cruncher comes in here. I'll give him a hair cut to remember! And it won't be just a little off the top!

22nd June, 1527

The Guv'nor has well and truly done it this time. He's asked for a divorce. Catherine can't believe it. It'll all end in tears, mark my words.

16th June, 1528

The Guv'nor has really got it in for Cardinal Cowpat these days. The cement had hardly dried on Wolsey's new house, Hampton Court, when the Guv'nor turned up.

"Hmm, nice place you've got here, Wolsey," he said. "Wouldn't mind living in it myself. It's a bit big for you, isn't it?"

Wolsey can pick up a hint. "Just what I was thinking, Your Majesty," he said. "It's yours."

"Oh, how kind. Ta very much. Close the door when you leave," said the Guv'nor. I'd have given a pound to see Cardinal Cowpat's face.

20th September, 1530

Still no royal divorce! The Guv'nor has given Cardinal Thomas Cowpat Wolsey the boot because he didn't manage to sort it out. I was hoping Wolsey would be brought straight to the Tower. So were the people who lined the Thames for a mile yelling for his blood, but the Guv'nor has decided to let him live for the moment. He's gone off to some monastery in Putney, with his tail between his legs.

Never mind, I can wait.

2nd December, 1530

I don't believe it; Cardinal Cowpat has cheated me after all!

He went up to York soon after he was kicked out. Then, when the Guv'nor told him to come back to London to be tried for treason, Wolsey lost his bottle completely. As he arrived in Leicester, he died!

Well, it can't be helped, but I'm sorry I never got to have a go at the old swine. He had such a lovely thick neck. Quite a challenge. I reckon I'd have had to get the saw out.

Wolsey.

16" neck 14" neck 10" neck 8" neck

15th March, 1531

Had to put the Bishop of Rochester's cook to death. Apparently he'd tried to poison Bishop Fisher by putting something in his soup. Luckily, the Bish didn't drink it but two people from his household did and they died, along with a few beggars who were also having a meal there. The court sentenced the cook to be stuck in boiling water.

Will Somers reckoned the beggars had been dying for something to eat. He also said we should throw some swedes and turnips in with the cook and make up a nice soup. If he's the country's top jester, I'd hate to hear the worst.

25th April, 1531

Got my own back on old Cruncher Harris today. He tried to mix doctoring and barbering once too often. The Guv'nor called him in to pull one of his teeth and Cruncher pulled the wrong one! Still, fair play to him, he was a laugh, old Cruncher. When he came to the block, he was laughing and joking just like always. "Just a light trim today, Chopper," he said.

"How short would you like it, Cruncher?" I said.

"Oh, just down to the shoulders," he said, putting his neck on the block. What a character! Joking right to the end.

I laughed his head off.

3rd May, 1531

The Guv'nor has had a cabinet reshuffle.
Sir Thomas More has been made Lord Chancellor.
More's a decent bloke; that's the trouble. He wrote
a book called *Utopia*, which is all about an ideal
country where everyone lives in peace and
harmony. He's honest, fair-minded, generous (as
long as you're not a Protestant), and about as in
touch with the real world as the Easter Bunny.
He'll be lucky if he lasts six months.

The other new member of the Guv'nor's
government is a fat toad called Thomas Cromwell.
His dad used to run the roughest pub in London.
He's a crafty so-and-so. That's why he'll last longer
than nice guy, Mr More.

Will Somers' latest joke is all the rage at court.
"When is a piece of wood like a king?...
When it's a ruler!"
Honestly!

7th July, 1531

The Church has decided that the Guv'nor is 'Protector and Supreme Head of the Church and Clergy of England'.

Cromwell's sorted it all out, of course, and the priests only agreed because he threatened to have their heads chopped off if they didn't. (I can't see the Holy St Thomas More standing for it, though.)

1st January, 1533

Anne Boleyn's been moaning for ages that she wants to be queen. The Guv'nor keeps telling her that the Pope won't let him divorce Catherine, and Anne always goes into a sulk.

When the Guv'nor popped in to wish me a Happy New Year, I could tell he had something on his mind. He told me Anne was expecting a baby. Oops, I thought, he's got a problem: he must marry Anne before the kid's born, especially if it's a boy. If Anne has a son before she marries the Guv'nor, the son couldn't be king. The Guv'nor's got one son already (that I know of) called Henry Fitzroy, but he can't be king because the Guv'nor never married his mum.

"What am I going to do, Chopper?" he asked.

I said I'd think about it.

8th January, 1533

I told the Guv'nor about my plan this morning. Well, both my plans in fact.

Plan number 1 – he makes his mate, Thomas Cranmer, Archbishop of Canterbury. If Cranmer gets to be judge in the divorce case, he'll find in favour of the Guv'nor.

The Guv'nor said that was all very well, but why would the Pope let Cranmer be judge? Aha, I said, that's where Plan number 2 comes in.

Plan number 2 – the Guv'nor makes himself Pope!

The Guv'nor blew a gasket, and asked if I'd gone stark ravin' mad? I explained he wouldn't have to be Pope of everywhere, just of England. The priests had already made him head of the Church, so he just needed to pass an Act of Parliament to make it Law. Then he could appoint Cranmer to judge his divorce case.

I thought it was a brilliant idea. The Guv'nor wasn't sure at first but he tried the idea out on Cromwell and, naturally, Cromwell was all for it. So now Cromwell will claim that the whole idea was his in the first place and cop all the credit.

Typical!

ye Sonne

Your Soarawaye Sonne

26th January, 1533   Still only Twelve Groats

Exclusive! KING REMARRIES!

Anne Boleyn Pregnant!

Ye Sonne can exclusively reveale that King Henry has secretly married Anne Boleyn, the recently created Marquess of Pembroke!

The weddinge tooke place just before dawn in the King's Private Chapel of Whitehall.

There were only four or five *Five actually, including me.* witnesses presente. Rumours have been rife about the state of the King's marriage. Royal watchers saye that Big Henry has not seen Queen Catherine for eighteen months and has been living in sinne with Anne Boleyn for some time.

Though the King has beene seeking a divorce, nobody expected this marriage to happen so soone.

Why Now?

A well-informed source says that Anne Boleyn is *that* pregnante and the King *reporter* wishes to have the childe *for this!* born legally! *I'll kill*

Should Anne Boleyn be Queene?

Ring Ye Sonne hotline
Dial 111 for yes
and 222 for noe

58

27th January, 1533

The Guv'nor wasn't too impressed with yesterday's front page story, so I had the *Sonne* reporter in today. He was supposed to be given the rack treatment to get him to say who spilt the beans about the Guv'nor and Anne Boleyn.

Well, I didn't need to torture him to find out, did I? I gave him the chop before he could say, "You know who it was, Chopper, it was you."

Sometimes the position of King's executioner is very useful!

30th March, 1533

Plan number 1 complete! The Guv'nor has announced that Thomas Cranmer is the new Archbishop of Canterbury.

AN ACTE RESTRAINING APPEALS TO ROME

Aprille 1533

Be it knowne that King Henry VIII of England decrees that:

1) England is an Empire.
2) The King is the Head of the Empire.
3) What he sayeth, goeth.
4) No foreigners (especially the Pope) can tell him what to do.
5) No one (especially Catherine of Aragon) is allowed to appeal for justice to the Pope, even in religious cases (and **Definitely** not in the case of her divorce).

Signed by us, **Henry Rex,**
in the 24th year of our reigne

(and Plan number 2 complete!)

ye Sonne

Your Soarawaye Sonne

15th April, 1533   Still only Thirteen Groats

MORE OUT, CROMWELL IN!

The Lord Chancellor, Sir Thomas More, resigned today. He said, "I wish to spende more time with my familie."

The real reason for Sir Thomas's resignation is thought to be in protest at the King's break with the Church of Rome, and the Act of Appeal that will make King Henry head honcho of the Church in England.

Political fixer and hard man, Thomas Cromwell, is the obvious candidate to replace More.

Sources close to the King say he is not pleased with his ex-Chancellor's criticism.

Ye Sonne says, "Keep your head, Sir Thomas – if you can!"

61

23rd May, 1533

The Guv'nor is dead pleased with himself. His divorce has finally come through and that's the end of it for poor old Queen Cath. Twenty-four years married to the Guv'nor, and now she's told she was never legally his wife. She's not Queen any more, though she's allowed to call herself Dowager Princess of Wales (big deal), and that sulky little sourpuss, Mary, is now Lady Mary, not Princess.

I can't help feeling sorry for Catherine; we've never seen eye to eye, but she was a good missus to the Guv'nor, except she didn't give him any sons.

1st June, 1533

Well, we had Queen Anne's coronation yesterday. The Guv'nor did his best to put on a good do, but it was a shambles. People didn't like Catherine much when she was Queen, but it turns out they like Anne Boleyn a lot less. No one cheered for her as she was driven to the Abbey, even though Will Somers did his best to get the crowd going. This could mean trouble...

ye Sonne

Your Soarawaye Sonne

11th July, 1533   Still only Sixteen Groats

RIGHT ROYAL MARRIAGE MIX-UP!

Pope Clement III said todaye that King Henry's marriage to Catherine of Aragon is LEGAL and his marriage to Anne Boleyn is ILLEGAL. He's also ordered that Henry should start to live with Catherine againe! If he doesn't then he will be excommunicated.

King Henry was not available for comment, but a close source ← *Me again!* says he is hopping *mad* and will ignore this ruling.

ye Sonne supports His Majesty and says, "Go home, Rome!"

7th September, 1533

I could hear the Guv'nor coming half a mile away. He came bursting into the armoury, chucking shields and pikes around, kicking armour. I just got a bottle out and waited for him to calm down.

"Another girl then, is it?" I said.

That set him off again. I can understand why. He'd gone to a lot of trouble to get a male heir, and his new Queen has let him down, just like his old one did. That's how it looks to the Guv'nor anyway. If I was Queen Anne Boleyn, I'd be worried sick. He's got rid of one wife already...

It was difficult for him to get rid of Catherine because she had powerful connections, but Anne hasn't a friend in the world – even her own family can't stand her. She'd better produce a son for Henry soon or the Guv'nor will decide she's got to go. He'll look for some way quicker than divorce, too.

Met the Royal Nursemaid out walking the new
Princess. They've decided to call her Elizabeth. I
must say she doesn't look as ugly as her half-sister,
Mary, but that's not saying much.

ye Sonne

Your Soarawaye Sonne

24th March, 1534   Still only Sixteen Groats

The penalty will be death

HAL HITS BACK!

Yesterday Parliament passed the Act of Succession, which states that the crown of England will pass to the children of King Henry and Queen Anne.

Anyone sayinge anything against the marriage of Henry and Anne or against their children who will be the lawful heirs, will from todaye be guiltie of treason!

The penalty will be death and all goods and lands forfeited.

All the King's subjects will also have to swear an oath that "they shall truly, firmly, constantly, without fraud or guile, observe, fulfil, maintain, defend and keep the whole effect and contents of this act". Anyone failing to sweare the Oath of Loyalty will be charged with treason.

Ye Sonne says, "That'll show the moaninge minnies. Your Majesty!"

20th April, 1534

Had to go up to Tyburn today to do a job – a mass hanging and beheading. Elizabeth Barton (alias the Nun of Kent), a couple of monks and three priests have been saying some nasty things about the Guv'nor's marriage. For instance, they said the Guv'nor would die within a month if he married Anne Boleyn. Well, he hasn't has he? Too bad for them.

People said that the nun went into trances and rolled around on the ground groaning, seeing visions of angels.

Well, now it's just her head rolling around on the ground and she'll be seeing angels for real.

25th April, 1534

Talk about busy! The Tower's full of people who don't want to take the Oath of Loyalty. Even Sir Thomas More is here! I had a chat with him today. He's a nice bloke with a sense of humour. I said I was sorry that it wasn't very comfortable in the Tower, so he said he wasn't complaining and I should throw him out if he did!

He wears a hair shirt and occasionally whips himself to show how religious he is. When he was in power, he used to send us loads of Protestant heretics for burning.

I told him he had nothing to worry about, as he was a mate of the Guv'nor's. He still didn't look very happy.

3rd July, 1534

The King's been off hunting deer, so there's not much going on around the Tower, apart from Will Somers annoying me.

"What do you call a deer with no eyes?" he asked.

"No idea," I said.

"Correct! No-eye-deer!"

I just stared at him.

"And what do you call a deer with no eyes and no legs?"

I shook my head. "Still no idea," I said.

"Correct. You must have heard it before."

I hate his jokes!

Christmas, 1534

The Guv'nor nipped in today to wish me a Happy Christmas. He said, just between him and me, he was getting a bit fed up with his new wife. There was no sign of her giving him a son. He was thinking of getting rid of her.

"I might even send her to you, Chopper," he said.

We had a laugh about that, but I wonder...

20th January, 1535

I haven't been paid for a couple of weeks so I mentioned it to the Guv'nor when he came in. He said he was sorry but he was a bit short of dosh, what with all his palaces to keep, the wars he'd had, his clothes and armour, etc. He said he didn't know what to do.

I had a bit of a brain wave. "Why not close down the monasteries?" I asked.

The Guv'nor wanted to know why that would help, so I made him a list of reasons:

i The church is rolling in money.

ii All the monks and nuns still think that the Bishop of Rome (formerly the Pope) should be head of our English Church.

iii They're a lazy bunch of loafers who have never done an honest day's work in their lives. All they do is kneel around all day wearing holes in their habits.

iv They're not supposed to have girlfriends or wives, but I've heard lots of stories about monks being caught with women.

v Once the monasteries are closed, the King can take all the lands and property that used to belong to them.

The Guv'nor liked the last bit, all right. He said Cromwell could become Vicar-General and could then organize an inspection of all the monasteries to find out loads of bad things about them. He could then close them down. It was the sort of job Cromwell would love!

I bet he would, I thought. I'm not keen to do creepy Cromwell any favours, but at least I might get paid on time.

4th June, 1535

Frying tonight! The Guv'nor sent us fourteen Protestant heretics to burn. You'd think the Guv'nor would be on the Prots' side; after all, he's always arguing with the Catholic Church.

On the other hand, I suppose that's just business: he still wants to let the Prots know that, although he's the head of the English Church, he's still a Catholic.

Religion! It's a complicated game.

19th June, 1535

Choppin' time again. Ex-Bishop Fisher has been found guilty of high treason for not recognizing the Guv'nor as the supreme head of the Church.

Also had three Carthusian monks today. Hung, drawn and quartered. Will Somers said they deserved it as they'd got into bad habits.

22nd June, 1535

I had to go up to Tower Hill to sort out ex-Bish
Fisher. He was dressed in his best clobber and put
on a good show. He made a pretty speech about
dying to preserve the honour of God. There wasn't
a dry eye in the house. Then he slipped me a few
groats to ensure it was a clean stroke. I would have
done my best to give him a
quick send off anyway, but
I'm not one to look a gift
horse in the mouth.

I went to have a few
beers at the inn afterwards –
killing 76-year-olds isn't
fun. A lot of people are
blaming Queen Anne.
She's getting very
unpopular.

1st July, 1535

Poor old Sir Thomas More has been found guilty
of high treason at Westminster for not taking the
Oath. I don't fancy choppin' Sir Thomas: I like the
bloke. Still, I dare say the Guv'nor will give him a
pardon.

7th July, 1535

Had to take off Sir Thomas More's head yesterday, at Tower Hill.

For the first time since I'd taken the job, I couldn't bring myself to chop him. He saw me hesitating and said, "Pluck up thy spirits, man, and be not afraid: my neck is very short."

Well, it was, and soon after that it was even shorter.

The Guv'nor was with the Queen when I went to report. She'd never liked Sir Thomas and she clapped her hands in glee and joked, "So it's Sir Thomas No-More."

I saw the look the Guv'nor gave her. Even Will Somers didn't laugh.

Well, mistress Anne, I thought, you may like executions now, but you might not be so keen on them before long.

20th November, 1535

I've been whiling away the long winter evenings by getting my little black book of the Guv'nor's girlfriends up to date. I have to keep it dead secret, because if the Guv'nor ever finds out about it, I'm dead.

Chopper's List
of Henry's Girlfriends
Top Secret
Not to be Read by Anybody

1510 ANNE HASTINGS

With Queen Catherine expecting a baby, the Guv'nor has been looking at certain ladies at court. Anne Hastings caught his eye! However, as soon as George, her hubby, got to know about it, he carted her off to a convent!

1514 JANE POPYNGCORT
what a pretty name!

The Guv'nor has been seeing her for a bit of a fling. She used to be the Duc De Longueville's mistress, when he was a prisoner of war, but now he's gone back to France, well...

1519 ELIZABETH 'BESSIE' BLOUNT

The Guv's had a son. But not a legal one! Elizabeth's married to Gilbert Tailboys, the son of old Mad Lord Kyme. The Guv'nor's keeping Gilbert quiet by making him a knight! He's calling the child Henry Fitzroy and making him Duke of Richmond.

What a shame Catherine hasn't had a son – she was upset when the Guv paraded the kid around court, I can tell you.

78

1525 MARY BOLEYN

She's been in France where she had an affair with the French king but she's recently married William Carey. Henry's decided that she is for him...

1526 ANNE BOLEYN

Now he's seeing Mary's sister! What a man!

Guv'nor 4 Madge

1535 MADGE SHELTON

The Guv'nor's been seeing Madge Shelton, Queen Anne's cousin and lady-in-waiting. I reckon that Queen Anne arranged this herself to stay in the Guv'nor's good books! Mind you from what the Guv said to me, Queen Anne's annoyed now it's happened!

7th January, 1536

11th January, 1536

The Guv'nor and the whole court are going round dressed in yellow. I thought they were celebrating the death of the Guv'nor's ex-missus, but Cromwell told me that in Spain yellow is the colour of royal mourning. The Guv'nor's made everyone wear it to avoid upsetting the Holy Roman Emperor (he's Catherine's nephew after all). So, as a mark of respect, everyone looks like an oversized banana. Mind you, there have been a few parties over the last few days as well; I reckon the Guv'nor is happy that Catherine's out of the way at last. He'd be dancing on her grave if he could do it without upsetting Emperor Charles.

ye Sonne

Your Soarawaye Sonne

20th February, 1536   Still only Seventeen Groats

JOBLESS TOTAL UP!

Up to 200 monasteries are to go across the countrie, with hundreds of monks and nuns to be made jobless.

Monasteries whose landes and property are worth less than £200 are to be closed down by order of King Henry and his Vicar-General, Thomas Cromwell.

In recent visits inspectors found

- Widespread Corruption
- Hypocrisy
- Traitors still loyal to Rome

Landes and buildings are to become crowne property, as are all precious items, metals, pictures and anything of worth. The treasury expects to receive thousandes of pounds from the closure.

A Spokesmonk said, "It's just privatization gone crazy with more money going to the people who've got too much already!"

Schools that are run by the monks will also have to close. The King has promised the building of more grammar schools to make up the loss. These will be called King's schools.

Although the larger monasteries have escaped, there are rumours (strongly denied) that the King aims to close these in the next four years. If so, 9,000 jobs will be lost as all 800 of England's religious houses are dissolved.

3rd April, 1536

The Guv'nor's a bit worried. He's getting totally fed up with Anne Boleyn. (I told him not to marry her – any woman with an extra finger on her hand and three breasts is bound to be trouble!) Anyway, she has not given him a male heir and it's rumoured that she's seeing someone else! (I should know, I started the rumours.)

So the Guv popped in for a quick chat.

Guv'nor: **Chopper, what would you do?**

Me: *No doubt about it. Chop 'er 'ead off. A short trial, find her guilty of messing around with other blokes, then a quick chopping trip.*

Guv'nor: I reckon you're right, Chopper. When could you fit her in?

Me: *(looking at my diary)* How does three weeks on Friday suit you?

Guv'nor: Can it be sooner, 'cos I fancy Jane Seymour?

Me: I know it's you, Guv'nor, but I'm fully booked. Look, I'll have a word with a mate from France, who's a dab hand with a two-handed sword, I reckon he'll be able to sort somethin' out.

Guv'nor: Thanks, Chopper, much appreciated.

Me: A pleasure, Guv'nor.

I also didn't fancy being someone who cuts off the head of the Queen of England. Not good for the public image!

17th May, 1536

Well, it was a short trial and they found her guilty (what a surprise!).

I did Anne's brother and his mates this morning. The Guv'nor had 'em topped at the Tower on purpose, so Anne could watch from her window. Very thoughtful of him.

The Guv'nor also got Cranmer to declare his marriage to Anne illegal, so little Elizabeth won't be Queen after all.

18th May, 1536

Complete bodge-up this morning. Anne was supposed to get the chop at nine o'clock, but nine came and went and there was no sign of the executioner. I was just thinking I'd have to do it after all when we got a message that the bloke had been held up on the Dover Road (honestly, traffic these days!). Apparently he'd said he would be here by noon, but by half past twelve there was still no sign of him so we had to postpone the execution until tomorrow.

19th May, 1536

The executioner from France finally turned up.
There was a good crowd – three thousand or so. I'll
give Anne her due; she gave a good speech. Then
the French bloke chopped her (nice sword
technique) and held up her head. She'd been
praying while she put her neck on the block and
her lips were still moving. I'd seen that happen
before, it's just a nervous reaction, but people started
muttering that she was a witch, and she was putting a
curse on them. It was getting a bit dodgy, with the
crowd looking as though they might start a
stampede, so I thought I'd lighten things up a bit.

I held her head up by the hair and said, "Gig us a
gottle of geer!" but nobody laughed. I'm wasted in
this job.

As for the Guv'nor, he's been throwing parties
all over the place and looking forward to marrying
Jane Seymour. Wonder how long she'll last?

21st May, 1536

Went to the Swan and Boar Inn. Only it isn't called that any more. It's been renamed. Will Somers organized it.

It's now called the Queen's Head.

30th May, 1536

I'll say this for the Guv'nor, he doesn't hang about! He got married again today, only eleven days after Anne got the chop!

Anne had to wait seven years for the crown, but Jane only had to wait seven months. Anne was queen for three years, so if the Guv'nor runs true to form and gets rid of Jane as fast as he got married to her, I reckon she's got about three months.

The latest Will Somers joke:
Question: Why did Anne Boleyn get the chop?
Answer: Because she couldn't afford the steak.
The Guv'nor thinks this is hilarious!

19th August, 1537

What a summer. No lying on a beach for me!

The Guv'nor asked me if I wanted a working holiday as he'd been having trouble with a load of Northerners. Apparently, they didn't like what the Guv'nor was doing to the monasteries so they decided to have a bit of a rebellion. They called it the 'Pilgrimage of Grace', but I don't know who Grace was. Well, obviously this annoyed the Guv'nor so I had to go to York and Lincoln for a bit of hanging, chopping and burning.

Talk about busy! I've done two hundred and sixteen at the last count! The Guv'nor told me not to hang or chop the two leaders, John Constable and Robert Aske, but to think of something to set an example. I hung them in chains from the city gates until they died of starvation.

The Guv'nor liked that.

1st September, 1537

After all the chopping I had to do in York, I reckoned it was about time I got an apprentice. I mentioned it to the Guv'nor who said he'd see what he could do.

I'd almost forgotten about it when Cromwell turned up this morning with a young lad in tow. He looked a right dodgy piece of work with a nasty twist to his mouth and shifty eyes. I didn't like the look of him at all. He said his name was Wilfrid Gumboyle. "Hard luck," I said.

Cromwell told me young Master Wilfrid used to be a monk but his monastery was dissolved, so he'd asked if there were any jobs going. Cromwell thought he wouldn't be interested in chopping people, with him being a monk and everything, but he said he didn't mind.

I bet he didn't. From the look of him, Master Wilfrid Gumboyle was the sort of lad who spent his entire boyhood pulling the legs off frogs.

Still, you can't get the staff these days. I said I'd take him on.

ye Sonne

Your Soarawaye Sonne

12th October, 1537   Still only Eighteen Groats

IT'S A BOY!

Aftere a long and difficult labour, the Queen was this day delivered of a bouncing baby boy. England at last has a male heir to the throne.

His Majesty, King Henry told our reporter, "I'm over the moon. At the end of the day, this is the result I've been looking for."

Some of the boys came round last night to celebrate the birth of young Prince Ed. It was one hell of a party – have I got a headache this morning!

Wilfrid said that he had the best cure for headaches.

"What's that?" I said. He just picked up the axe, stroked it lovingly and smiled. I reckon I'd better keep a close eye on him!

13th October, 1537

What a day! All the bells in London have been ringing non-stop, there have been bonfires in the streets, parties all over the place and the gunners in the Tower only stopped firing salutes when the cannon melted.

The Guv'nor invited me over to Hampton Court to see the new Prince, which was nice of him. The fuss they made of that kid, you'd think he was made of china, but I can understand why – if anything happened to him, the Guv'nor would be right back where he started.

Anyway, I did my bit of who's-a-good-ickle-boy-ing and left them to it. The Queen seemed a bit off-colour but I suppose giving birth can do that.

24th October, 1537

Queen Jane died early this morning. The Guv'nor told the Duke of Norfolk to arrange the funeral and dashed off to Windsor. He can't stand anything to do with death, which is a bit odd when you think how much of it he's caused.

25th April, 1539

That little greaser, Cromwell, is very full of himself at the moment. He's got Parliament to pass an Act to close down the rest of the monasteries, so that's loads-a-dosh for the Guv'nor (and for Cromwell, too, if I know him).

Will Somers came over to tell me his latest riddle.

"What's got a neck, but no head?" he asked.

"You, after I've given you the chop," I said, hopefully.

"No, the correct answer is a bottle," he replied.

"I prefer my answer," I said, stroking my axe.

He left very quickly.

10th January, 1540

Flippin' 'eck! Someone's for the chop!

I've just seen the Guv'nor's new wife – Anne of Cleves! Talk about ugly! Last time I saw a face like that, it had a ring through its nose.

Cromwell sent the painter, Hans Holbein, to paint a few portraits of continental ladies so the Guv'nor could choose his new Queen. Well, I reckon I could have done better myself with a squirrel's tail and a pot of whitewash!

Holbein painted five different portraits and showed them to the Guv'nor. The Guv'nor reckoned that Anne of Cleves was the best looking one, so he got Cromwell to sign him up to marry her.

Everything was fine until Anne arrived in England and the Guv'nor met her. I can assure you, Henry is NOT happy.

"If this was beauty, what was ugliness!" he's been going round saying. And having seen her, I reckon he's right! He's already calling her the Flanders Mare and the rumour I've heard... well, let's just say I don't think we'll be seeing another royal Prince or Princess from Queen Anne!

The Guv'nor's not in a good mood and he's been blaming Cromwell for the mess. I reckon that I might be seeing Mr Holbein and Mr Cromwell very soon!

15th April, 1540

As Will Somers said, the Guv'nor keeps chopping and changing his mind – and his wives!

He popped down this morning and when I'd got rid of Wilfrid by sending him off to find a left - handed axe, he told me what he was planning. He's going to get rid of Cromwell because Cromwell made him marry Anne of Cleves. He's also going to get a divorce because he's met some woman called Catherine Howard and he fancies her something rotten.

"What do you reckon, Chopper?" he asked

I said, "Good idea, Guv. About time you had a change. And you know me, I'm all for beheadings and a funeral."

And I'm making my axe especially blunt for Mr Cromwell!

10th June, 1540

Cromwell turned up to work this morning as usual to find a warrant for his arrest for treason. He was absolutely gobsmacked.

When they brought him to the Tower, he looked like a bloke who was having a nightmare and couldn't wake up. Serves him right. He's sent a lot of people to their deaths on false charges. Let's see how he likes it.

11th July, 1540

Anne has wisely agreed to a divorce. She'd obviously rather lose her crown than her head. In fact, from what I've seen of her, she seems a sensible woman, not a bit like that bubble-head, Catherine Howard.

28th July, 1540

What a day! A wedding and a funeral. I had to wear my best togs for the Guv'nor's marriage to Catherine Howard, and then change into the leathers and nip back to Tower Hill for a real treat – taking Cromwell's top off!

Apparently he'd written to the Guv'nor asking for mercy – the Guv'nor showed me the letter. "Most gracious Prince, I cry for mercy, mercy, mercy!"

Honestly, what a coward!

The Guv'nor winked at me and said "No mercy, Chopper."

It took me two strokes of the axe to finish the job. My axe wasn't sharp enough. Funny that!

No mercy, Chopper!

4th December, 1540

I'll say this for Queen Catherine; she's put new life into the Guv'nor. He's frisking about like a spring lamb. Up at five, church at seven, then he goes out with his hawks until dinner at ten. Not bad for a bloke with a fifty-four inch waist! Of course, he wouldn't be so fat if he didn't eat like a pig.

28th May, 1541

Wilfrid's first chopping! I knew it would be a shambles, and I was right. Wilfrid's a bloodthirsty little swine but he's got no experience. He volunteered to chop Lady Salisbury, who was sixty-eight if she was a day. When this poor little white-haired old granny put her neck on the block, he went to pieces. He muffed his first swing and panicked. Chop, chop, chop all over the place.

Well, you can imagine the mess.

30th October, 1541

The Guv'nor sent for me this evening. When I went in, he was sitting holding a letter, just staring at nothing. I asked him what was up and he gave me the letter to read. It was from Cranmer. It said that Catherine had been having an affair with Francis Dereham.

Here we go again...

7th November, 1541

I was walking to the Chapel with the Guv'nor when there was a great commotion. The Queen came flying down the corridor calling for the Guv'nor to wait and listen. Before she could say anything, a load of guards caught her and dragged her off, screaming the place down (the Queen was screaming, not the guards). I think she reckoned if she could get the Guv'nor on his own she could talk him round. He thinks so as well, which is why he won't see her.

I've been doing some investigating, and I reckon this time the Queen's accusers are right. Dereham isn't the only bloke she's been carrying on with, from what I hear. Stupid girl! I'm afraid she's going to be put on my chopping list.

Ye list
(chopping.)

3rd September. 1510
Sir Richard Empson
Edmund Dudley
15th September. 1513
Edmund de le Pole
17th May. 1521

10th December, 1541

Had to do the Queen's lovers today. Thomas Culpeper had admitted adultery. He wasn't allowed the block, but I was kind to the bloke – I lopped his head straight off, clean as a whistle, as he knelt on the ground.

Dereham wouldn't admit adultery so he got the full treatment. I left the disembowelling to Wilfrid; it's the sort of thing he likes.

ye Sonne

Your Soarawaye Sonne

16th February, 1542   Still only Nineteen Groats

FIVE DOWN! HOW MANY TO GO?

King Henry's fifth wife, Catherine Howard, got the chop today. As she was brought to Traitor's Gate by boat last Saturday, she passed beneath the mouldering heads of her former lovers, Culpeper and Dereham, which still hang over London Bridge.

The former queen admitted her crimes and said she deserved a hundred deaths.

Then the executioner removed her head with one stroke.

When King Francis I heard about Catherine's behaviour, he told Ye Sonne correspondent he was shocked. "Je suis shocked," said French Frank. "Zutalors! She has done wondrous naughty."

18th December, 1542

The Guv'nor's decided to take his temper out on the Scots. He sent an army up there last month, and they beat the Scottish army in a battle at Solway Moss. Apparently, King James V was so upset he took to his bed and died, so his baby daughter (born the same day) is now Mary, Queen of Scots. The Guv'nor wants her to marry his son, Edward, but there's no hurry. After all, Edward's only five. I hope she likes older men.

16th February, 1543

The Guv'nor's in love again, with another
Catherine: Catherine Parr. This is good news – and
bad news.

Bad News – She's not all that young.

Good News – She's younger than the Guv'nor.

Bad News – She's already married.

Good News – Her husband's sick and will
probably die.

Bad News – She's in love with a bloke called
Thomas Seymour.

Good News – Thomas Seymour works for the
Guv'nor.

So all the Guv'nor has to do is wait for Catherine's
husband to die, send Seymour off on a diplomatic
mission to Timbuktu and, Bob's your uncle – wife
number six.

Ye Sonne

Your Soarawaye Sonne

12th July, 1545   Still only Twentie Groats

CRAZY KING WEDS WIFE NO. 6

Half-witted Henry, the Mad Monarch of Multiple Marriages, has done it again! Today he tied the knot with his SIXTH wife, Catherine Parr.

In case Ye Sonne readers have forgotten, the dotty despot's five previous wives were:

Catherine of Aragon	*Divorced*	*1509 - 1533*
Anne Boleyn	*Beheaded*	*1533 - 1536*
Jane Seymour	*Died*	*1536 - 1537*
Anne of Cleves	*Divorced*	*1540 - 1540*
Catherine Howard	*Beheaded*	*1540 - 1542*

Will wife no. 6 get on any better than the other five?

Ye Sonne says, "Leave it out, Henry. Enough's enough."

The Guv'nor showed me the paper this morning. He also told me to go and see the editor and have a quiet word with him.

14th July, 1543

I took my axe and had a quiet word with the editor of *Ye Sonne*, and then gave his widow a few crowns to be getting on with.

8th July, 1544

The Guv'nor's off to France. He's already had another go at the Scots, and now fancies a crack at Francis, so he's going to attack Boulogne. If you ask me, he just wants to bring back some cheap booze.

He's told everyone Catherine is in charge while he's away.

I'll admit I had my doubts about her, but she's turning out to be just what the doctor ordered. She even gets on with Guv'nor's daughters. Well, I quite like Elizabeth myself, but the Queen even likes Mary! I didn't think it was possible.

30th September, 1544

The Guv'nor landed at Dover today, having captured Boulogne and has come back with the spoils of victory – and loads of duty-frees. The Queen went to meet him, and they really seemed pleased to see each other. Maybe this time the Guv'nor has got it right.

ye Sonne

Your Soarawaye Sonne

20th July, 1545   Still only Twentie-one Groats

THE MARY ROSE: DOWN SHE GOES!

The great warship, the Mary Rose, sank yesterday afternoone in Portsmouth harbour, right before King Henry's eyes!

The Mary Rose was part of a fleete of 80 ships gathered to stop a French invasion force.

During the morning, the French fleete had been chased off by our great navy. But then tragedy struck! As the Mary Rose returned to Portsmouth harbour, she suddenly capsized and sank.

Nearly all the 500 crew were drowned, including the Vice Admiral of the Fleet, Sir George Carey. It is thought that only 30 survived.

Lucky Escape

Earlier in the day, the King had dined on board the Mary Rose, but luckily had left the vessel when news of the French fleet's attack reached him.

Why Did the Ship Sink?

One expert says that there could have been a number of possible reasons:

- Too many people on board
- Too many heavy guns
- Too many people standing on one side of the ship.

The King has ordered that a salvage operation to raise the ship should begin. He wants to rescue the ship's guns. Italian contractors have been called in already.

Fat chance. I was there and I saw the whole thing. The Guv'nor was crying his eyes out and I wasn't so far off crying myself. He'll never get the ship up though: it's one of the biggest he had – it must weigh thousands of tons. I reckon it'll still be down there in four hundred years.

24th December, 1545

The Guv'nor's been taken ill again. He's never really been well since the *Mary Rose* went down. He had an attack in March, but this is worse. The doctors are useless; they can't do a thing for him. Even Will Somers can't cheer him up with his bad jokes.

Doesn't look like being much of a merry Christmas at court, this year.

18th June, 1546

My heart's not in this job any more.

The Guv'nor doesn't seem interested in anything these days. He's got so fat, we had to rig up a hoist to get him up and down the stairs, and another to get him into and out of bed. Servants have to carry him everywhere.

Without the Guv'nor in control, everyone at court is trying to get power. Young Wilfrid has become very pally with the Howards, who blame me for executing Catherine. He's after my job, is young Wilfrid, and if the Guv'nor dies – and he doesn't look too good to me – I reckon I'll be for it.

Had to burn another heretic today – young woman called Anne Askew. I don't mind chopping people for proper reasons like murder and treason, but chopping somebody just because they don't agree with someone's view on religion isn't right.

So before we lit the fire, I hung a bag of gunpowder round her neck to make it quick. And, it was, but when we had to hand the body back to her family for burial it took us half the night to find all the bits.

12th December, 1546

Well, we've got distinguished company in the Tower tonight – The Duke of Norfolk (Catherine Howard's uncle) and the Earl of Surrey (her cousin).

Serves them right. They tried to get rid of the Queen by telling the Guv'nor she wanted to turn England into a Protestant country. Luckily, some fool dropped the warrant for her arrest and she found out what was going on. She managed to talk the Guv'nor round before she got the chop.

I'm looking forward to doing Norfolk and Surrey. I can't think of two blokes who deserve chopping more.

30th December, 1546

The Guv'nor made his will tonight and got me to witness it. Leaving out all the legal jargon, it says that Prince Edward gets to be King after the Guv'nor. (He's only nine so he'll have to have some of the Earls to advise him.) If Edward dies, Mary will be Queen (gawd help us!), and if she dies, it'll be Elizabeth.

The Guv'nor wants to be buried beside Jane Seymour, and Catherine gets all his property.

I witnessed the will and told the Guv'nor not to worry; he'd got years in him yet. But I know he hasn't, and so does he.

19th January, 1547

Chopped the Earl of Surrey today. I thought Wilfrid might make himself scarce as he's supposed to be a mate of Surrey's, but he was there all right, and if he shed any tears it must have been while I wasn't looking.

28th January, 1547

The Guv'nor called me into his chamber last night. I knew he was dying. He was very weak, but he asked me to send a letter to King Francis which he'd written a few days ago. I hope it gets there before Francis pegs out as he's on his last legs, too. Funny when you think they've been rivals all their lives and now it looks as if they'll die within a few days of each other.

Then the Guv'nor said, "D'you know why I chose you to be my executioner, Chopper?"

I'd always wondered.

He said, "I found out we had the same birthday. We were both born on 28th June 1491. Bet you never knew that."

Well, I didn't. He never gave me a present, mean old devil.

Anyway I'd brought him the Duke of Norfolk's death warrant, but seeing him lying there, I couldn't bring myself to ask him to sign it.

He said, "I'm dying, Chopper." And I said, "I know, Guv'nor."

He asked me to send for Cranmer, so I did, and Cranmer was with him when he died this morning at two o'clock.

15th February, 1547

Something spooky happened last night. The Guv'nor's coffin had been bounced around a fair bit on its last journey to the chapel at Windsor Castle, and it split open. Some blood from the body dripped out, and a dog came trotting in and licked it up.

I remembered when the Guv'nor sent Catherine of Aragon away, a Spanish priest had said, "He should be as Ahab, and the dogs would lick his blood." It made me cold all over.

When I got back to the Tower, young Wilfrid was waiting for me. He was being very considerate: had I had a good journey? Would I like to warm my feet? How about some sack? All very suspicious.

The Duke of Norfolk has got friends at court who know I've got Norfolk's death warrant. I don't like the way young Wilfrid's looking at me. I don't like it at all.

This is the last entry in the Diaries of 'Chopper' Smith, but when they were found, a small piece of paper was discovered inside one of the notebooks in different handwriting:

> I have founde the Mafter's private dyarie. Yt is a thousande pitties I did notte discovere it soonere, for My Lorde of Norfolke woulde have rewardede me greatlee to have it putte into his hande, butte I maye stille hope to mayke use of itte to send my Maftere to the blockke and secure hys position for myselfe.

It seems likely from this that the despised Wilfrid Gumboyle finally got the better of his employer after all.

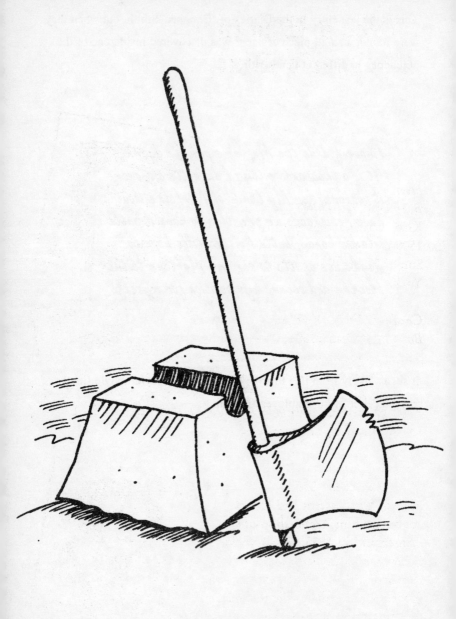

Who's Who in Chopper's Diary

Henry VIII
Born 1491 *Died* 1547
King of England and Wales from
1509 to 1547.
Son of Henry VII and Elizabeth of
York.

Cardinal Thomas Wolsey
Born 1474 *Died* 1530
Son of an Ipswich butcher, he became
a priest and rose through the ranks.
Henry made him Lord Chancellor in
1515. He became Archbishop of York
and was later made a Cardinal.

Thomas Cranmer
Born 1489 *Died* 1556
He was a Protestant and Henry
appointed him Archbishop of
Canterbury in 1533. He survived
Henry and compiled the *Book of
Common Prayer*. When the Catholic
Queen Mary came to the throne she
had him burnt at the stake.

Thomas Cromwell
Born c.1485 *Died* 1540
Son of a blacksmith and innkeeper.
Like Wolsey, he rose in the ranks and
was appointed Chancellor. Helped
organize the royal divorce and the
dissolution of the monasteries.
Executed in 1540.

Sir Charles Brandon
Born 1484 *Died* 1545
The son of Henry VII's standard
bearer. A great soldier and supposedly
the best jouster in England. Henry
made him Earl of Suffolk in 1514. He
married Henry's sister, Mary.

Sir Thomas More
Born c.1477 *Died* 1535
A devout Catholic scholar who was
made Chancellor of England by
Henry. He refused to swear an oath
agreeing that Henry was the head of
the Church. He was accused of
treason and beheaded in 1535.

Will Somers
Dates unknown
Henry VIII's chief fool. He was
introduced to Henry in 1525 and
remained his loyal servant throughout
Henry's life.

Catherine of Aragon
Born 1485 *Died* 1536
Daughter of Ferdinand and Isabella of
Spain. Henry's first wife. Married June
11th, 1509. Divorced March 30th, 1533.

Anne Boleyn
Born c.1504 *Died* 1536
Daughter of Sir Thomas Boleyn and
Elizabeth Howard. Henry's second
wife. Married 1533. Executed 1536.

Jane Seymour
Born c.1509 *Died* 1537
Daughter of Sir John Seymour. Henry's
third wife. Married 1536. Died 1537, 11
days after giving birth to Edward.

Anne of Cleves
Born 1515 *Died* 1557
German daughter of John, Duke of
Cleves. Henry's fourth wife. Married
1540. Divorced six months later.
She outlived Henry.

Catherine Howard
Born date unknown *Died* 1542
Daughter of Lord Edmund Howard.
Henry's fifth wife. Married 1540.
Executed 1542.

Catherine Parr
Born 1512 *Died* 1548
Daughter of Sir Thomas Parr of Kendal. Henry's sixth wife. Married 1543. She outlived Henry and married former boyfriend, Lord Thomas Seymour. She died in childbirth.

Mary Tudor
Born 1516 *Died* 1558
Daughter of Henry VIII and Catherine of Aragon. Became Queen on Edward VI's death. She had hundreds of Protestants executed during her reign. This led to her being known as Bloody Mary.

Elizabeth Tudor
Born 1533 *Died* 1603
Daughter of Henry VIII and Anne Boleyn. She became Queen Elizabeth I after the death of Mary. She remained unmarried and has gone down in history as one of the greatest English monarchs.

Edward Tudor
Born 1537 *Died* 1553
Son of Henry VIII and Jane Seymour. On the death of Henry, he became Edward VI at the age of ten. He suffered ill health and died at the age of 16.

PUBLISHER'S ADDENDUM

Although all the facts contained in this diary are more or less correct,
it has been brought to our attention that there are several mistakes,
which raises the question of the diaries' authenticity.

- There is no mention of Chopper Smith in any official
  documentation of the time
- If Chopper did exist it is highly unlikely that he would have been
  able to write, as nearly all men of his social class would have been
  illiterate in Tudor times
- There are no records of a daily newspaper in Tudor England,
  particularly not one called Ye S o n n e , and if it ever existed it
  certainly didn't have a telephone hotline!
- The Reformation of Religion and the dissolution of the
  monasteries was Cromwell's idea. No-one has ever suggested that
  an executioner would have been involved in deciding policy in
  Henry VIII's court!

Although the two men who found the diaries, Steve Barlow and Steve
Skidmore, had them authenticated, there is no record of the two so-
called notable historians they asked. From this, and other evidence, it
would appear that the diary and cuttings are forgeries. The Publishers
wish to apologize. They request that if you see the two suspects, please
inform them or the authorities immediately.

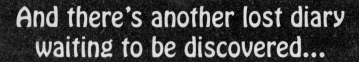